Olympia
the Games
Fairy

Special thanks to Narinder Dhami

No part of this work may be reproduced, stored in a retrieval system, or transmitted in any form or by any means, electronic, mechanical, photocopying, recording, or otherwise, without written permission of the publisher. For information regarding permission, write to Rainbow Magic Limited, c/o HIT Entertainment, 830 South Greenville Avenue, Allen, TX 75002-3320.

ISBN 978-0-545-45703-3

12 11 10 9 8 7 6 5 4 3 2 1   12 13 14 15 16 17/0

Printed in the U.S.A.   40
First Scholastic printing, May 2012

Olympia
the Games
Fairy

by Daisy Meadows

SCHOLASTIC INC.

New York   Toronto   London   Auckland
Sydney   Mexico City   New Delhi   Hong Kong

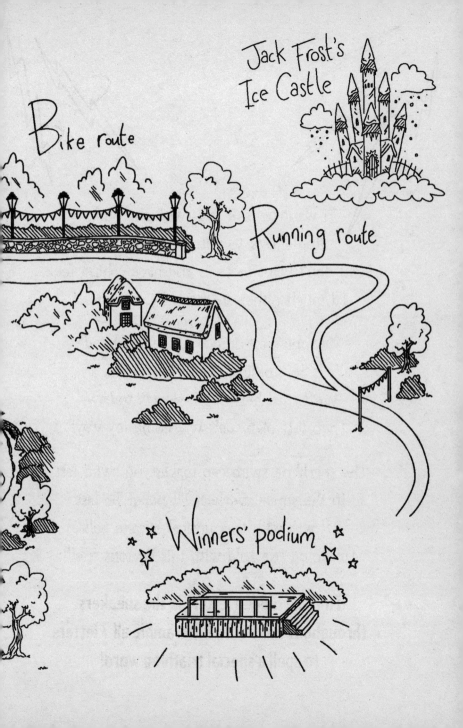

I want to bike and swim and run,
And I have to win or it's no fun!
But I don't want to train and have aching feet,
I'd much rather steal and lie and cheat!

Olympia's magic can give me a hand,
So, goblins, off to Fairyland!
We'll steal her magic objects today—
Then lots of medals will come my way!

The sparkling swim cap makes you swim fast,
In the super sneakers I'll never be last.
I'll win with the musical bicycle bell,
I'm going for gold with this devious spell!

Find the hidden letters in the sneakers throughout this book. Unscramble all 7 letters to spell a special triathlon word!

The Sparkling
Swim Cap

Contents

Swimming Surprise

"This is going to be so exciting!" Kirsty Tate said, beaming at her best friend, Rachel Walker. Kirsty had just arrived in Tippington to stay with Rachel for part of the summer. "It's the first time I've ever been to a—" Kirsty stopped, looking confused. "*What* did you say this sporting event was called, Rachel?"

Her friend laughed. "A triathlon," she reminded Kirsty as Mr. Walker turned the car down a street marked TO THE RIVER. "All the athletes take part in swimming, biking, and running races, one after the other. They don't even get a break in between! That's right, isn't it, Mom?"

"Yes," replied Mrs. Walker from the passenger seat. "They go from one event right to the next."

Kirsty's eyes opened wide. "Wow, they must be in good shape!" she exclaimed.

"I think we're going to be exhausted from just cheering them on," joked Mr. Walker, who was searching for an empty space in the packed parking lot.

The triathlon was taking place in the pretty riverside town of Melford, not far from Tippington. As they all climbed out of the car, Kirsty admired the little thatched cottages and the stone church with its square bell tower. It was a perfect summer day! The sky was bright blue, and the sun beamed down.

"There are so many people here," Rachel remarked as they followed the crowd down the street. Up ahead, the girls could see a waterfront area with an old stone bridge spanning the wide river. A set of steps led down to the edge of the river. There, men and women in bathing suits and bright swim caps were standing on the steps, waiting eagerly for the race to start. A big crowd had already gathered. There were spectators sitting on wooden

bleachers, and some were also standing
on the bridge.

"How far do
they have to
swim?" asked
Kirsty.

"See that
yellow buoy

bobbing around farther down the river?"
Mrs. Walker pointed it out to the girls.
"The athletes swim around that and
come back to where they are now. It's
about a half mile, or 750 meters."

"And then they dry themselves off and
jump on their bikes for the next part of
the triathlon," Rachel's dad added.

Nearby was a roped-off area where
there were racks of bicycles with helmets

hanging on the
handlebars.
"The bike
race is about
twelve and
a half miles
long."

"Oh, I'm getting tired just thinking about it!" Kirsty sighed, making Rachel laugh.

"Ladies and gentlemen," boomed a voice from a loudspeaker attached to one of the lampposts, "the Melford Triathlon will begin in five minutes! Will all the competitors take their starting positions, please?"

Rachel and Kirsty watched as the swimmers got into position at the bottom of the steps. The girls also noticed some

small boats bobbing around nearby.
They were manned by people in white
baseball hats with MELFORD TRIATHLON
written on the front in blue. Rachel
guessed that it was their job to make sure
the events ran smoothly.

"Mom, could Kirsty and I watch from the riverbank?" asked Rachel eagerly. "Then we can get a *really* good view of the race."

Her mom nodded. "We'll see you back here later," she told them. "Then we can go and have an ice tea at one of the cafes in Melford."

While Mr. and Mrs. Walker found some seats in the bleachers, Kirsty and Rachel hurried along the waterfront to an empty spot near a clump of reeds.

"Isn't this magical?" Kirsty remarked. Sunbeams glinted on the water, and the

girls could see
shimmering
blue and
green
dragonflies
dancing
across the
surface.

"Speaking of
magic, I wonder if we'll see our fairy
friends this summer," Rachel said with a
smile.

"Oh, I hope so!" Kirsty exclaimed, her
eyes lighting up. She and Rachel loved
being secret friends with the fairies.
They'd had some amazing magical
adventures together.

Just then, there was the sound of a
whistle, followed by loud splashes as all

the swimmers plunged into the river.
There were cheers from the crowd, and
Rachel and Kirsty joined in.

But as the swimmers moved toward the
yellow buoy, something very strange
happened. Half of the athletes spun
around in the water and began heading
in the *opposite* direction! Almost all of the
other competitors started swimming

around and around in circles without
going anywhere at all.

"What's happening, Rachel?" Kirsty
asked, looking confused.

"I guess it might have something to do
with the currents in the river," Rachel
said. "But they wouldn't be *this* bad!"

The people on the riverbank had
stopped cheering and were now
murmuring to one another in surprise.

Everyone stared in amazement as the swimmers bumped into one another. Their arms and legs were getting all tangled up!

"Look at that boat, Kirsty," Rachel said. "It's making things even worse!"

Kirsty saw that one of the boats was floating around the swimmers, getting in their way and making everything even more chaotic.

"I thought those people were supposed to be *helping*!" Kirsty said as the boat chugged past some of the swimmers,

forcing them to move out of its way.

A sparkle on the surface of the river suddenly caught Rachel's eye, and she nudged Kirsty.

"There's one swimmer who seems OK," Rachel said. She pointed across the water. "See that boy, Kirsty? The one in the shiny swim cap?"

Kirsty shaded her eyes from the sun and saw one of the swimmers powering

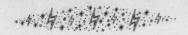

through the water
toward the
yellow
buoy.
The
sunlight
was reflecting
off his
dazzling
silver swim
cap.

"I wonder how
he can swim in the right direction when
everyone else is having trouble." Kirsty
said with a frown.

"I think that boat's trying to catch up
with him," said Rachel. The boat had
managed to get free of the crowd of
swimmers, and it was now sailing toward

the one in the sparkly cap. At that moment, there was another announcement over the loudspeaker.

"Attention, everyone!" it boomed. "Due to unusual currents in the river, the race will be postponed while the organizers check things out."

Rachel and Kirsty glanced at each other in disappointment.

"Oh, I feel so sorry for all the swimmers!" Kirsty sighed.

"I bet the boy in the shiny swim cap

isn't too happy," Rachel said. "He was really far in the lead!"

As the girls watched, the officials began to lower dinghies from their boats to pick up the floundering swimmers. As she waited to see what would happen next, Rachel noticed something very unusual. The clump of tall green reeds next to them was glowing with an amazing golden light.

"Kirsty!" Rachel whispered, nudging her friend. "See that? I think it really *is* magic!"

As Rachel spoke, a tiny glittering fairy peeked out from behind the reeds.

"Hello, girls," she called as Rachel and Kirsty both caught their breath in excitement. "I'm Olympia the Games Fairy!"

Games and Goblins!

Olympia flew over to the girls, fluttering from reed to reed so that no one in the crowd would spot her. Finally she came to rest on the riverbank. The girls sat down on the grass so that they could talk to her without being seen. Her golden hair sparkled in the sunlight and she was wearing a red running outfit with a blue warm-up jacket over it.

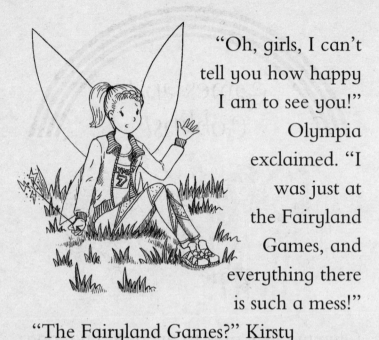

"Oh, girls, I can't tell you how happy I am to see you!" Olympia exclaimed. "I was just at the Fairyland Games, and everything there is such a mess!"

"The Fairyland Games?" Kirsty repeated. "What are those, Olympia?"

"We have swimming, biking, and running events," Olympia explained, "just like you're watching here today. It's my responsibility to look after *all* tournaments in the human and the fairy worlds."

"You mean like this triathlon?" asked Rachel.

Olympia nodded. "I have three magical objects to help me," she explained. "The sparkling swim cap makes all swimming events safe and fun. Then there's my musical bicycle bell—that ensures that bike races run smoothly. And the super sneakers make sure that all running events are successful."

"So what happened at the Fairyland Games?" Kirsty wanted to know.

"Well, the swimming event was just

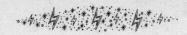

about to start," Olympia said with a sigh, "but when the competitors dove into the water, they all began swimming in circles or heading in the wrong direction! And that's when I discovered that my sparkling swim cap was missing."

Kirsty and Rachel exchanged excited glances.

"That's exactly what happened here, too, Olympia," Rachel told her. "But everyone thinks the currents in the river are causing the swimmers' problems."

Olympia looked worried. "I have to

find the sparkling
swim cap," she
murmured
anxiously. "If
I don't, the
swimming events
at the human and

fairy games will be ruined!"

"Did Jack Frost and his goblins steal
your sparkling swim cap, Olympia?"
asked Kirsty. Whenever there was a
problem in Fairyland, it was usually
because of cold-hearted Jack Frost and
his naughty goblins. "Are they up to their
old tricks again?"

"I'm not sure," Olympia replied slowly.
"There *were* some goblins hanging
around watching the Fairyland Games.
I overheard them talking about sneaking

off to the human world to have some fun, so I followed them here. I don't know if they have the sparkling swim cap, but I can feel that it's somewhere close by!"

"We'll help you look for it," Rachel suggested. "I don't think the race will start again for a while."

Kirsty, Rachel, and Olympia glanced across the water. The officials' boats were still picking up swimmers. Most of the swimmers had been rescued by now, and Kirsty could see that the only one left splashing around in the water was the boy in the shiny swim cap. The boat that had caused all the chaos earlier was now almost even with him. The boy's silver swim cap was glittering in the sunlight. As he raised his head from the water to

look up at the boat, Kirsty caught a glimpse of a long green nose. Shocked, she clapped her hand over her mouth.

"Olympia, I can see a goblin in the water," Kirsty said, "and I think he's wearing your sparkling swim cap!"

Dragonfly Disguise

Olympia took a long look at the lone swimmer in the water, and then her face broke into a huge smile.

"You're right, Kirsty," she declared. "Nice job!"

"What now?" asked Rachel. "We need to get the sparkling swim cap from that goblin! But how?"

"I'll turn you into fairies," Olympia decided. "Then we can fly out to the goblin and try to grab the cap before the boat picks him up. Does that sound like a good plan?"

"That's a great idea," Kirsty replied.

Rachel looked a little worried. "There are a lot of people here to watch the triathlon," she pointed out. "What if someone sees us?"

"I've already thought of that," Olympia replied with a grin. "See all the dragonflies fluttering over the surface of the water? Well, we're going to be dragonflies, too!"

Olympia pointed her wand at Kirsty and Rachel, and a mist of magical fairy dust surrounded them. The girls felt themselves shrinking down so quickly that it left them breathless! In just a few seconds, they were the exact same size as Olympia. Kirsty and Rachel each had their own pair of delicate fairy wings on their backs. But as they fluttered up into the air with Olympia, the girls saw that with every movement,

all their wings glittered with shiny blue and green metallic sparkles.

"My fairy magic made us a dragonfly disguise!" Olympia laughed. "Now let's go and stop that goblin from getting away with my sparkling swim cap!"

Olympia zoomed off across the river, and Rachel and Kirsty followed. They flew as fast as they could, skimming the surface of the water and dodging around the real dragonflies on the way. But they weren't quite fast enough! Ahead, they could see that the officials' boat had

already reached the goblin swimmer.

"Oh, no!" Olympia exclaimed as they flew closer. "Look, girls! Those people on the boat are goblins, too. See the big green ears poking out from under their baseball hats?"

Rachel's heart sank as she realized that Olympia was right. Two of the goblins on the boat were struggling to untie the dinghy, while the third and biggest goblin was leaning over the side, shouting at the swimmer.

"It's *my* turn to wear the sparkling swim cap now," the big goblin yelled. "Hand it over!"

The goblin swimmer was treading water, looking annoyed. "No way!" he muttered.

The big goblin glared at him. Suddenly, he reached over the side and pulled the sparkling swim cap right off the other goblin's head!

"Give that back!" the swimming goblin howled as Olympia, Rachel, and Kirsty hovered silently above them. The other

two goblins on the boat saw what was happening. They abandoned the dinghy and rushed over to the big goblin.

"*I* want to wear the sparkling swim cap!" one of them roared, trying to grab it from him.

"No, me!" the other shrieked. Meanwhile, the goblin in the water was climbing up the side of the boat. He jumped onto the deck and tried to snatch the sparkling swim cap back from the big

goblin. As all four
goblins fought over it,
the swim cap slipped
from their fingers
and flew over the
side of the boat.
It fell into the
river with a
splash, then
bobbed up and
down in the water.

"Come on!" Olympia whispered to
Rachel and Kirsty. "Now's our chance!"

"You fools!" the big goblin shouted.
"Quick, someone dive in and get it!"

Olympia, Rachel, and Kirsty swooped
down to the water, their eyes fixed on
the sparkling swim cap. They were
determined to get it before the goblins

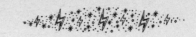

did. But then Kirsty spotted a sleek
brown shape gliding silently through the
water. It was an otter—and it was
heading straight for the sparkling swim
cap!

With one smooth movement, it
grabbed the cap in its teeth, turned
around, and swam off again.

Inside the Otter's Den

"Oh, no!" Olympia cried. "Girls, we have to follow that otter!"

The three friends flew after the otter, skimming low across the surface of the water. Behind them, they could hear the goblins grumbling and groaning, all blaming one another for losing the sparkling swim cap.

"I wonder why the otter wants a swim cap," Rachel said. The otter was swimming toward the opposite bank of the river with the sparkling swim cap still clutched firmly in its mouth.

"I have no idea," Olympia admitted. "I just hope we can persuade the otter to give it back!"

The otter reached the riverbank. She scrambled out of the water and slipped out of sight into a hole among the tree roots.

"She went into her holt," said Olympia, fluttering around outside the

hole. "That's what an otter's home is
called. We'll have to follow her inside."
She put a finger to her lips. "We need to
be very quiet, because we don't want to
scare her."

Rachel and Kirsty nodded. Olympia
flew into the holt, and the girls followed
her.

It was dark inside, but Olympia used
her magic to light their way. As they
flew through some interconnected
passages, Kirsty was impressed by how
well-made the holt was.

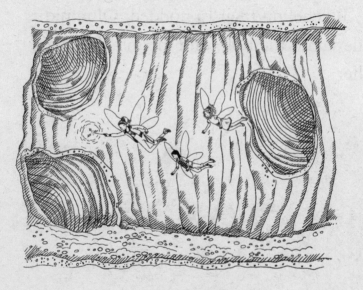

Suddenly, the three friends saw a faint
silver light ahead of them. They had
reached a big central chamber at the
heart of the otter's den!

The otter was laying the sparkling
swim cap on the ground and smoothing
it out with her paws. Olympia, Rachel,
and Kirsty smiled when they saw five
adorable baby otters curled up in a ball
together, watching their mother with big
brown eyes.

"Come along, children," the otter said.
"I've found you a nice, cozy new bed!"
She patted the swim cap with her paw.

Rachel fluttered forward. "Excuse me," she said politely.

The otter looked around in surprise, and all the babies stared at Rachel.

"We're very sorry to bother you," Rachel went on, "but I'm afraid that swim cap was stolen from our friend Olympia here. She would really like it back!"

"The sparkling swim cap is *very* important," Kirsty chimed in. "Its magic

helps swimming events at games and tournaments run smoothly. There will be chaos without it!"

"I'm sorry," the otter replied, "but it's taken me forever to find my babies a comfy bed. I don't want to give it up!"

Olympia's Lullaby

"Oh, no!" Olympia murmured.

"Olympia, listen," Rachel whispered in her ear. "What if you used your magic to make an extra-special bed for the otter's babies?"

"Great idea!" Kirsty agreed, and Olympia nodded.

 "We can see that you just want a nice, soft bed for your cute babies," Olympia told the otter. "So if you give us the swim cap back, I'll use my magic to make the coziest, softest, and most comfortable bed in the whole world!"

Rachel, Kirsty, and Olympia stared hopefully at the otter. What would she say?

The otter thought about it for a few seconds.

"That's very nice of you," she said at last, her whiskers twitching a little. "You can have the swim cap back."

Beaming, Olympia flew over to the sparkling swim cap. The otters watched, wide-eyed, as she tapped the cap with her wand. Magical sparkles immediately returned it to its Fairyland size! Olympia picked up the sparkling swim cap and tucked it safely under her arm.

"Thank you so much," Olympia said to the otter. "And now I'll keep my part of our deal!"

Olympia waved her wand and sang:

Close your eyes, sleepyheads,
And lie down in your cozy bed.
Snuggle down, all warm and dry,
And listen to my lullaby.

As Rachel, Kirsty, and the otters
watched, a mist of magical fairy dust
floated down from Olympia's wand and
landed on the ground. Immediately,
a large circular nest appeared, made
of moss, grass, leaves, and feathers. The

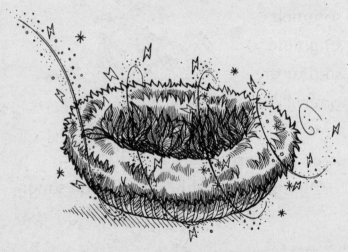

little otters gave squeaks of delight and scampered over to climb inside.

"That's a wonderful nest," the mother otter said gratefully. "Thank you."

"Good-bye!" called Olympia and the girls, waving as they flew out of the holt.

"And sweet dreams!" Kirsty added.

Outside, Olympia, Rachel, and Kirsty

gazed out across the river. They were all glad to see that the goblins' boat had vanished.

"Girls, thank you so much for your help," Olympia said with a huge smile. "I have to rush the sparkling swim cap back to Fairyland now, so that the swimming event can go on as planned."

"Can Kirsty and I stay fairies for a little while?" Rachel asked. "We'll get a great view of all the triathlon events from high up in the air!"

"And we can keep an eye on those goblins, too," Kirsty added.

"Of course," Olympia agreed. "I'll come back later and change you back to your human size. Good-bye, girls!"

"See you soon," Rachel and Kirsty chorused as Olympia disappeared in a flurry of magical sparkles.

As the girls skimmed across the water, back to

the other side of the river, they heard another announcement booming over the loudspeaker.

"Attention, everyone! The currents are now back to normal. The swimming race will restart in five minutes."

"Whew!" Rachel said happily. "We've managed to keep the first event of the day from being a total disaster!"

"Yes, but I wonder where those troublemaking goblins have gone?" Kirsty replied. "I bet we haven't seen the last of them!"

The Musical
Bicycle Bell

Contents

Bicycle Breakdown

"Wasn't that amazing?" Rachel said with a huge grin. She and Kirsty applauded along with the rest of the excited crowd.

The swimming race had just ended. The girls had loved watching the thrilling finish, with three of the swimmers fighting it out for first place. Now those

three swimmers were out of the water, drying themselves off as quickly as they could and pulling on their bike shorts and helmets. They were getting ready for the bicycle race! Other competitors were running out of the river as they completed their swims.

"If the bike race is as exciting as the swimming, it'll be amazing!" Kirsty declared. She and Rachel were still fairy-size, perched on a  windowsill high up on one of the houses. The house was on the street that led to the river, and it was right at the beginning of the bike route.

"We'll have a great view, and no one will notice us up here," Rachel said. "They'll be too busy watching the race!"

The girls leaned forward eagerly as the

first athlete climbed onto his bike. Head down, he pedaled off with a determined look on his face. But he'd only gone a few feet when his bike began to wobble wildly from side to side. "What's happening to my handlebars?" he cried, looking bewildered. He came to a stop—and then held his handlebars up in the air. They'd become completely detached from his bicycle!

"Oh, that's terrible," Kirsty said to Rachel. "Look, the other two are going to pass him."

The swimmers who'd finished second

and third were on their bikes now, too. They both sped off, only to stop abruptly with shouts of dismay! The front wheel had come off one of the bicycles and was rolling away down the street. The chain had come loose from the other bike, and was dragging on the ground.

"What's going on?" Rachel murmured, watching carefully.

Most of the swimmers were pedaling off on their bicycles now, but none of them got more than a few feet before

something went wrong. Seats began to
fall off the bikes and crash to the ground.
Wheels, chains, and handlebars came
loose. Some of the bicycles even started
to go backward, even though the cyclists
were all pedaling forward.

The crowd looked on in amazement as the competitors came to a stop and got off their bikes, one by one. It was a complete mess!

"Attention, everyone!" The announcer, whose voice boomed over the loudspeaker, sounded just as surprised as everyone else. "In the interest of safety, the race has been stopped for an investigation. It will begin again in ten minutes."

"I hope they give the swimmers who came in first a head start," Kirsty remarked. "It won't be very fair otherwise."

"I'll bet this has something to do with those awful goblins," Rachel said thoughtfully.

"I think you're right, Rachel!" Kirsty replied, her face lighting up with excitement. "Look!"

Kirsty pointed at the loudspeaker on the corner of the street. Rachel saw dazzling golden sparkles drifting out of it, and she smiled.

"Olympia's back!" Rachel announced as the fairy flew out of the front of the speaker. She waved at the girls and then zoomed toward them.

Kirsty noticed that their friend looked

very worried. "Did something happen in Fairyland, Olympia?" she asked.

"Because the bike race here is in complete chaos!" Rachel added.

Olympia sighed. "Some of the goblins thought it would be fun to steal my musical bicycle bell!" she explained. "That's why *all* cycling events have been disrupted—including the one that's about to start in Fairyland. Will you help me find the bell?"

"Of course we will!" Kirsty and Rachel cried.

Super Cyclists!

Olympia looked relieved. "Thank you so much, girls," she replied. Then she glanced down the street. All of the cyclists were gathered in a big group, trying to fix their bikes with help from the officials.

"I think we should move away from here," Olympia went on. "Since there's no bike race to watch right now, someone might glance up and spot us."

"The race route goes that way," Kirsty said, pointing around a corner. "Should we fly down one of these other roads? There won't be any crowds waiting there."

"Good idea," Olympia agreed.

 Making sure to fly high up in the air and stay close to the houses, the three friends flew quickly along the street. Then

they turned the corner and flew down
one of the side roads. Kirsty was right.
The road was empty because it wasn't
part of the race route.

"We can still see what's going on,"
Rachel said as they landed on
top of a lamppost. She
pointed down the road.
Main Street was down
that way, and they
could see some of
the crowd waiting
patiently for the
race to restart.

"We'll fly back
to join the
crowd as soon
as the race
begins," Olympia promised.

"I know the goblins must be around here *somewhere*. They'll be super cyclists now that they have the musical bicycle bell, so I'm sure that they'll want to be in the race!"

"When did the goblins steal the bell, Olympia?" asked Kirsty.

"Just before the Fairyland bicycle race was about to start," Olympia told her, frowning. "Stacey the Soccer Fairy saw them running off with it."

Rachel was still gazing at the crowd down on Main Street. Suddenly, she saw five cyclists dressed in brightly colored

shirts, shorts, and helmets slip out into the street from behind the crowd. They zoomed off on their bikes, heading for the road where Rachel, Kirsty, and Olympia were hiding.

"Why are those cyclists coming down here?" Rachel wondered. "The race

doesn't go this way. And, besides, it hasn't even restarted yet!"

"Maybe they're having their own race?" Kirsty suggested.

The cyclists were pedaling very fast, speeding down the road. As they got close to the lamppost where Olympia and the girls were sitting, one of the cyclists bashed into another one and knocked his helmet off. The friends gasped—his head was green!

"Goblins!" Kirsty whispered.

At that moment, the goblin in the lead rang the silver bell on the front of his

bicycle. A beautiful melody filled the air. Rachel and Kirsty could see very faint sparkles of fairy magic drifting around the bell.

"That goblin has my musical bicycle bell on his handlebars!" Olympia cried. "After him, girls!"

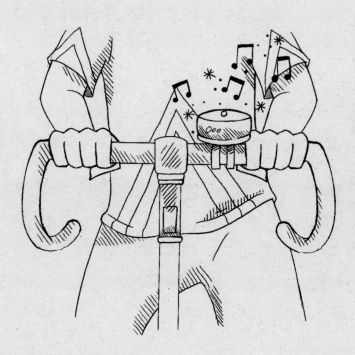

Grab That Bell!

Olympia, Rachel, and Kirsty fluttered
down from the lamppost. They chased
the goblins, who were still pedaling so
fast that their big green feet were just a
blur.

"Do you think we can catch them and
get the bell back?" Rachel whispered.

The goblins were so fast, it was hard for
Olympia and the girls to keep up with
them.

"I'm not sure," Olympia murmured.
"But we can't let them out of our sight,
whatever we do!"

Kirsty realized that the goblins were
racing on the empty streets that weren't
part of the bike route. That was lucky!
There was no one around on those streets
to see them.

The goblin with Olympia's bell rang it again as he raced around the next corner.

"You've had the musical bicycle bell for a long time," one of the other goblins complained, panting as he cycled along. "Let someone else have a turn—like me!"

"*I* want the bell!" puffed the goblin whose helmet had fallen off. He'd stopped to pick it up, and now he was at the back of the pack. "It's *my* turn!"

"Fine, then come and get it!" the first goblin jeered. He turned to stick his tongue out at the others, and then pedaled off as fast as he could.

The other goblins followed, still yelling and complaining.

"You know Jack Frost wants the silly magic bell so that we can win the bike race," shouted the second goblin. "So you'd better not lose it!"

"Yes, Jack Frost is *really* mad that the fairies got the sparkling swim cap back

again," the
last goblin
reminded
them.
"He was
hoping one
of us would
win the
race. He
wants to win
everything!"

"So Jack Frost
told his goblins to steal my bell so that
one of them can cheat and win the
bicycle race!" Olympia murmured.
"Girls, we have to find a way to stop
them!"

The goblins were still biking around the
empty streets. Even though Olympia,

Rachel, and Kirsty flew as fast as they could, they weren't able to catch up with the goblins. Before long, Rachel realized that they'd gone around in a big circle and were almost back where they'd started. The goblins were close to the official race route again! They were heading toward the busy streets packed with people waiting to watch the race.

"We'll be back near the crowd in a minute or two," Rachel pointed out, looking worried. The goblins turned the corner and were heading along the road where Olympia and the girls had first spotted them.

"They're going straight toward Main Street," said Olympia. "We won't be able to follow them there — someone might see us!"

"What are we going to do?" Kirsty said desperately. "If the goblins join the race when it's almost finished, they'll win by cheating!"

The goblins were getting closer and closer to the crowd. All of a sudden, the goblin at the back of the pack bent down

from his bicycle and picked up a stick
lying in the road. As Olympia and the
girls watched, he pedaled hard and
caught up with the goblin in front. That
goblin was biking along smugly, loudly
ringing the musical bicycle bell over and
over again.

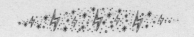

The goblin with the twig leaned over—and stuck it in the spokes of the first goblin's front wheel! The wheel stopped turning instantly, bringing the bike to a sudden stop. With a yell of surprise, the goblin let go of the musical bicycle bell and went flying over the handlebars. He landed in the road with a groan, and his bicycle crashed down next to him.

"This is our chance to grab my bell!" Olympia whispered.

But before Olympia, Rachel, and Kirsty could do anything, a race official who'd been standing on the corner rushed toward the goblins.

"What are you doing?" the official demanded with a frown. "The race hasn't restarted yet. You shouldn't be riding around here, anyway. It's not part of the route." He glared at the groaning goblin, who was dusting himself off. "And was that you, ringing your bell so loudly? That's against the rules, you know!"

The official bent down and removed the musical bicycle bell from the goblin's bike. "I'm going to hold on to this until the race is over!" the official said. Then he slipped Olympia's bell into his pocket and hurried off.

Noise Annoys!

"Oh, no!" Olympia gasped, horrified.
"What do we do now?"

"We'll just have to wait around.
Hopefully, we'll get a chance to take the
bell out of his pocket." Rachel sighed as
the official went back to his post at the
corner.

"But there are so many people around," Kirsty pointed out. "It's going to be *really* difficult to get to the bell now."

The goblins were arguing furiously with one another. "This is all your fault!" one of them screeched at the goblin who'd had the bell. "*You* lost the musical bicycle bell, and *you're* the one who's going to have to tell Jack Frost!"

"I wouldn't have lost it if this fool hadn't stuck a twig in my wheel," the goblin muttered, shoving the goblin who'd had the twig.

"Yes, you would have!"
the other one
retorted, shoving
him back.
"That official
said you're not
allowed to ring
your bike bell all
the time. He would
have taken it from
you, anyway! You
were just showing off because you had
the bell!"

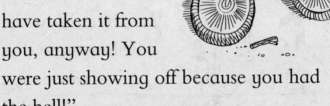

"You're a great big show-off!" the
other goblins chorused.

As the goblins continued to yell and
bicker, Kirsty racked her brain. There
had to be a way to get the musical
bicycle bell back without being seen.

"Oh!" she exclaimed suddenly. Rachel and Olympia glanced at her eagerly.

"Do you have an idea, Kirsty?" asked Olympia. The little fairy smiled hopefully.

Kirsty nodded. "We can't fly over to the official and take the bell without being seen," she said slowly. "But maybe we could make him throw the bell away so that we can get it back!"

"How?" asked Rachel.

"By making the bell ring and ring without stopping!" Kirsty turned to Olympia. "Could you do that

with your magic, Olympia?"

Olympia grinned and nodded. She pointed her wand at the race official, and a stream of magical sparkles danced through the air toward his pocket.

Immediately, the air filled with the clear and beautiful sound of the musical bicycle bell. The official jumped with surprise! Fishing inside his pocket, he pulled the bell out. Olympia and the girls watched as he tried to turn it off. No such luck!

The bell kept ringing loudly. Everyone in the crowd was looking at the official, wondering why he didn't just turn the bell off. Even the goblins had stopped arguing and were watching curiously.

The official stared down helplessly at
the musical bicycle bell as it rang on and
on. He shook it a few times. When it still
didn't stop, he looked around and spotted
a trash can behind him.
Quickly, he hurried over
and threw the musical
bicycle bell in the
garbage. Looking
very embarrassed,
he rushed
back to his
position.

"Hurry,
girls!" Olympia
whispered.
The garbage
can was behind the race official, who
now had his back to them. Silently

Olympia, Kirsty, and Rachel flew down toward it.

"Look out!" Kirsty gasped as she saw the goblins rushing over to the garbage can, too.

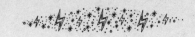

The musical bicycle bell was lying on top of the garbage in the can, and Olympia flew down to pick it up. But to Rachel and Kirsty's dismay, the goblins hurled themselves at the bin.

"Don't let them get it!" one of the goblins yelled.

The Race Begins

All the goblins stuck their arms into the
garbage can at the exact same moment,
and ended up banging their heads
together! As they cried out in pain,
Olympia swooped down between them
and grabbed the musical bicycle bell. The
instant Olympia touched the bell, it
stopped ringing and shrank down to
Fairyland size. Rachel and Kirsty sighed
with relief.

Olympia fluttered into the air with a big smile, clutching the bell. One goblin jumped up to try and catch her, but he accidentally knocked into the garbage can. The garbage flew everywhere! All the goblins shrieked with rage as they were covered in apple cores, candy wrappers, and other garbage.

"Give us back the bell!" one goblin roared furiously. Olympia shook her head as she, Rachel, and Kirsty hovered above the goblins. "Go home and tell Jack Frost

that he should learn how to be a good
sport instead of trying to win by
cheating!" she told them.

The goblins moved away from the mess
on the ground. They were complaining

so loudly that the official glanced around to see what was going on. As he did, Olympia, Rachel, and Kirsty zipped out of sight behind the garbage can.

"What are you doing *now*?" the official asked, shaking his head as he stared at the garbage-covered goblins. "You should be lining up, so you're ready when the race starts."

"Go away!" one of the goblins muttered. "We don't even want to be in the race now!"

Shaking themselves free of trash, they all slouched away, leaving their bikes behind.

"Girls, I can't thank you enough for all your help," Olympia declared, her eyes shining. "I was *so* worried we wouldn't be able to get my beautiful bell back. Then the bicycle races here and in Fairyland would both have been disasters!"

"Ladies and gentlemen," the announcer said over the

loudspeaker. "We are very happy to tell you that the bikes have been fixed and we can now restart the race. Will the cyclists get in position, please?"

"Oh, great!" Rachel exclaimed. "It looks like everything is back to normal."

"Girls, would you like to come back to Fairyland with me to return the musical bicycle bell?" asked Olympia. "Then you can stay and watch our bike race, too."

"We'd love to!" Kirsty agreed eagerly, and Rachel nodded.

Olympia waved her wand with a smile.
In the twinkling of an eye, all three of
them were swept up in a cloud of
glittering magic — and whisked away to
Fairyland!

The Super
Sneakers

Contents

Ready, Set, Stop!

Just a few seconds later, Olympia, Rachel, and Kirsty arrived at the outdoor stadium in Fairyland. King Oberon and Queen Titania were seated in the Royal Box, and the stadium was packed with fairies who were there to watch the races.

"Rachel and Kirsty helped me find the musical bicycle bell!" Olympia announced, holding up the bell. The fairies all cheered and applauded.

The girls watched as Olympia flew over to the Royal Box. At the front of the box were three pedestals: one bronze, one silver, and one gold.

Olympia carefully placed the musical bicycle bell on the bronze pedestal. Rachel and Kirsty could see the sparkling

swim cap on the
silver stand,
and on the
gold
pedestal
was a pair
of gold
sneakers.
They glittered
with fairy magic.

"Those must be
the super sneakers,"
Rachel said, as she and Kirsty admired
them. "They look amazing!"

"They're the sparkliest sneakers I've
ever seen!" Kirsty replied.

King Oberon and Queen Titania stood
up and waved to Rachel and Kirsty.

"Thank you, girls! Thank you,

Olympia!" King Oberon called. "We
had to delay our races because of those
goblins, but now we can continue."

"We're glad you're
here, Rachel and
Kirsty," Queen
Titania added
with a sweet
smile. "We
were just about
to start our
running race.
After that, we'll
hold the swimming and cycling races.
Please join us!"

The fairies in the stadium clapped
again as Olympia, Rachel, and Kirsty sat
down in the front row. Looking around,
Rachel could see lots of their old friends

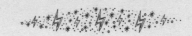

in the audience. She waved hello to India
the Moonstone Fairy, Crystal the Snow
Fairy, and Willow the Wednesday Fairy,
who were sitting nearby.

Then Bertram the
frog footman
stepped onto
the running
track.

"It is time
for the running
race to begin,"
Bertram
announced,
and there was
another burst
of cheering.

"Our contestants today are the Rainbow
Fairies!" the frog footman went on.

Delighted, Rachel turned to Kirsty as Ruby, Amber, Sunny, Fern, Sky, Inky, and Heather jogged onto the track. "There are lots of our fairy friends here," Rachel pointed out, "but the Rainbow Fairies are our *very* oldest fairy friends!"

Kirsty smiled. "We had our first magical adventure with them!" she remembered. "I wonder who's going to win? I'm going to cheer for all of them!"

The seven Rainbow Fairies went to the starting line. There was great excitement in the air as everyone, including Rachel

and Kirsty, leaned forward eagerly in
their seats to watch the race.

Bertram cleared his throat. "On your
mark!" he called.

The seven fairies got into position on
the track.

"Ready!" Bertram went on. "Set!" He paused. "GO!"

The Rainbow Fairies surged forward, and everyone in the stadium began to shout and cheer. But almost immediately, Ruby and Amber stumbled and fell at exactly the same time.

"Our laces are tied together!" Amber yelled. She and Ruby fumbled on the track, trying to untangle their shoelaces.

Meanwhile, Fern and Sky had stopped, too. They were both

hopping around, trying to pull their sneakers off. Rachel and Kirsty watched them anxiously. What was going on?

"My sneakers are too small!" Fern groaned.

"Mine, too," Sky agreed. "Ow! They're pinching my toes!"

Sunny, Inky, and Heather had run along the track, leaving the others behind. But then Sunny yelled in distress.

"Oh, no! My sneakers are too BIG!" she cried.

Rachel and Kirsty looked down at

Sunny's sneakers. They had become as
big as clown shoes! Sunny couldn't run in
them, and ended up falling over.

"Help!" Inky shrieked, coming to a
stop and staring down at her bare feet.
"My sneakers have disappeared!"

"And *one* of my sneakers has vanished, too," added Heather, hopping around on her remaining shoe.

Olympia frowned. "Everything's going all wrong!" she cried.

Keep on Running!

As Bertram and the other frog footmen
rushed to help the Rainbow Fairies,
Rachel saw another old friend hurrying
toward them. It was Samantha the
Swimming Fairy!

"Hello, girls!" she called, looking distressed. "Thank you so much for helping Olympia find the sparkling swim cap. I'm so glad the swimming race can go ahead. But now we have another problem!"

Samantha turned and pointed to the golden pedestal that stood underneath the Royal Box.

"The super sneakers are gone!" Kirsty exclaimed, her eyes wide with surprise

and alarm.
"But they were
there a
minute ago."
"So that's
why the
running race
is all mixed
up!" Olympia said, biting her lip. "Was
it the goblins again?"

Samantha shook her head. "No, it was
Jack Frost himself!" she explained. "He
snuck into the stadium. While everyone
was busy cheering and applauding, he
stole the sneakers—right before the race
started. I don't think anybody spotted
him except me."

Just then, King Oberon and Queen
Titania had been told that the super

sneakers were no longer on the golden
stand under the Royal Box. Some of the
fairies in the audience had also realized
that the sneakers were gone, and they
were murmuring anxiously to one
another.

"This is awful!" Olympia sighed,
looking completely devastated. "Jack
Frost is so sneaky! What do we do now?"

"Don't worry,
Olympia,"
Kirsty said,
comforting
her. "Rachel
and I will
help you get
the super
sneakers back."

"Of course we will," Rachel agreed. "I

bet Jack Frost took them to his Ice Castle!"

Olympia brightened up a little. "Your Majesties," she called, as she and the girls fluttered over to the Royal Box. "Jack Frost snuck into the stadium and stole the super sneakers, but Rachel, Kirsty, and I are determined to get them back!"

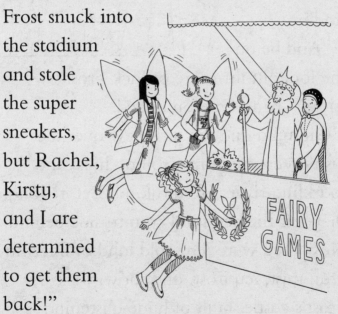

Cheers and whoops rang out around the stadium.

"Be careful, all of you," Queen Titania

cried, waving as
Olympia, Rachel,
and Kirsty
fluttered
out of the
stadium.

"And be on
the lookout for more of Jack Frost's
tricks!" King Oberon added.

Olympia and the girls flew over the
lush green meadows, rolling hills, and
sparkling rivers of Fairyland. Before long,
they left the beautiful countryside behind.
Now they were in a cold land of freezing
gray mist, icy frost, and snow. Jack
Frost's castle, built of huge glistening
blocks of ice, loomed up ahead of them
through the gloom. The girls had been to
the Ice Castle many times before, but

seeing it still sent a shiver down Rachel's spine.

"How are we going to get inside?" Kirsty asked as she, Olympia, and Rachel hovered near the entrance.

"I'm not sure," Olympia said. Then she gasped as the doors began to open. "Hide, girls—quickly!"

The three friends zoomed up and  ducked behind one of the castle's icy turrets. Then they peeked around the wall to see who was coming out.

To her surprise, Kirsty saw Jack Frost himself running out of the castle. He was

wearing a tank top and shorts — and on his feet were the super sneakers! Kirsty nudged Rachel and Olympia, pointing silently at Jack Frost's feet.

Jack Frost was followed by a crowd of his goblins. As he ran up and down outside the castle entrance, the goblins milled around him. They all looked worried.

"Do something!" Jack Frost roared furiously as he ran around in circles. "Anything!"

"What's going on?" Rachel whispered. The goblins were now running around in a panic, bumping into Jack Frost and one another.

"The powerful magic of my super sneakers means that Jack Frost can't stop running!" Olympia exclaimed with a giggle.

Stinking Sneakers!

Jack Frost ran frantically in a circle. His normally pale blue face was red, and he was panting hard.

"Get these stinking sneakers off my feet!" he bellowed at the panicking goblins. "NOW!"

"I have an idea!" a big goblin yelled. He gathered a couple of the others around him and whispered his plan to them. Then they all charged into the Ice Castle. A few minutes later, Olympia, Rachel, and Kirsty saw them come out carrying a large net.

"We're going to try and catch you," the goblin explained to Jack Frost.

"Well, hurry up!" Jack Frost shouted.

The goblins ran up to Jack Frost and tried to toss the net over him. But at the last moment, the super sneakers sent him

running away in the opposite direction.
Instead of capturing Jack Frost, the net
fell over some other goblins.

"Help!" shrieked a goblin caught in the
net. "Get us out of here!"

The big goblin freed the ones who were
trapped in the net, and then he and his
friends tried again to catch Jack Frost.

This time, though,
they managed to
tangle *themselves*
up in the net!
Olympia and
the girls giggled.

"You fools!"
Jack Frost
snarled as he
raced around
his Ice Castle.
"You're all in
big trouble now!"

"Let me help!" shouted a goblin with
big ears. As Jack Frost ran past him, he
leaped forward and tried to tackle him to

the ground. Unfortunately, another goblin had had the same idea—and he dove for Jack Frost at the exact same time. The goblins ended up tangled in a heap as Jack Frost sprinted away.

"STOP!" Jack Frost shrieked, glaring down at the super sneakers. "I order you to STOP!" But he continued to run around the Ice Castle at top speed.

"How are we going to get the sneakers back?" Rachel asked with a frown. "There doesn't seem to be any way to slow Jack Frost down!"

As Jack Frost ran toward the castle entrance again, he glanced up and spotted Olympia, Rachel, and Kirsty hovering above him. He gave a cry of rage.

"You fairies!" Jack Frost shouted furiously. "Come down here immediately and help me!"

"We will," Olympia agreed, "*if* you give back the super sneakers."

Jack Frost scowled. "No, no, NO!" he yelled. "I want to win *everything*, and you pesky fairies aren't going to stop me!" Then he pointed his ice wand at the sneakers, zapping them with his magic. "That won't work!" Olympia called. "You can't stop the super sneakers with just any old magic spell!" But Jack Frost ignored her and continued to try all his spells. Suddenly, he shrieked with surprise as an

ice bolt whisked him off his feet and out of sight.

"One of Jack Frost's spells has accidentally taken him back to the human world!" Olympia sighed, lifting her own wand. "Come on, girls, we have to follow him!"

A Very Strange Prize

With a wave of Olympia's wand, a burst of fairy magic carried the three friends back to Melford.

"Look, the bike race is over and the running race has already started," Rachel said as she, Olympia, and Kirsty looked down on Main Street. There was

a crowd of runners heading toward the
finish line. A small podium had been set
up there, ready for the awards ceremony.
There were three judges sitting nearby,
waiting to present the prizes.

"And there's Jack Frost!" Olympia
exclaimed,
pointing with
her wand.
"He appeared
right in the
middle of the
pack of
runners!"
Rachel and
Kirsty could
see Jack Frost
running along with
the other athletes. But then, to their

dismay, the runners
began
having
problems
with their
sneakers. They
stumbled,
tripped, or fell
over, just like

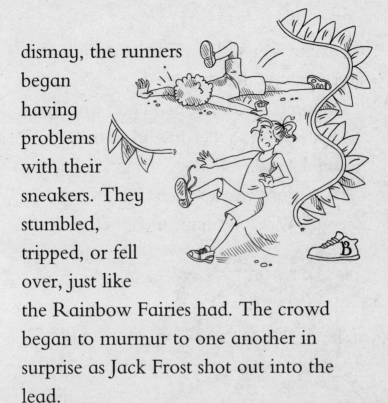

the Rainbow Fairies had. The crowd
began to murmur to one another in
surprise as Jack Frost shot out into the
lead.

"The race is almost over, and Jack
Frost is going to win!" Kirsty cried.
Jack Frost was sprinting toward the
finish line as the other runners struggled
after him.

"Maybe the organizers will stop the

race, like they did with the swimming
and cycling," Rachel said.

Olympia shook her head and frowned.
"I don't think so, because it's almost
finished," she replied.

"What are we going to do?" asked
Kirsty. "We don't have a chance of
grabbing
the super
sneakers with
all these
people
watching."
"Let's wait

for Jack Frost to collect his medal,"
Olympia suggested. "He'll go back to his
Ice Castle afterward, and we can follow
him."

Jack Frost was grinning widely and

waving at the crowd as he ran by. Arms in the air, he crossed the finish line and cheered in triumph. "I won!" Jack Frost bragged. "Hooray for me!"

"Only because you're wearing my super sneakers," Olympia muttered with a sigh. "You there!" One of the race organizers strode over to Jack Frost. "You're disqualified!"

Jack Frost looked furious. "Why?" he demanded, jogging in place as the other

runners began to limp and stumble across the finish line.

"Because you appeared in the middle of all the other runners right at the end!" the organizer snapped. "And you're not even wearing a number." He glared at Jack Frost. "You're disqualified!" he repeated and walked off.

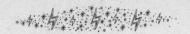

"Look at Jack Frost," Rachel whispered to Kirsty and Olympia. "He's really annoyed!"

Jack Frost looked awfully upset. He rushed over to the podium with the other competitors and ran furiously in place as one of the judges stepped up to the microphone.

"What an eventful triathlon this has been!" the judge said with a smile. The crowd laughed and applauded. "I'm happy to say that despite all the problems we've experienced today, this has been one of our best triathlons ever. Now we'll present our winners with their medals. . . ."

Kirsty saw Jack Frost scowl icily.

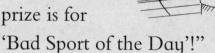

"But first, we have a very special prize to present," the judge went on. "The prize is for 'Bad Sport of the Day'!"

The crowd cheered.

"And our winner is the runner who appeared at the end of the race!" the judge went on. He pointed at Jack Frost. "Would you come and collect your prize, please?"

Jack Frost's face lit up. "I *am* a winner after all!" he yelled happily. He dashed forward and shook hands with the judge while running in place. The judge  solemnly handed Jack Frost a large, wilting green cabbage.

The crowd burst out laughing—and so did Olympia, Kirsty, and Rachel.

But Jack Frost was delighted! Clutching his cabbage, he ran down the steps again and down the street. "After him, girls!" Olympia whispered. Jack Frost had turned off of Main Street now and was jogging along one of the empty roads. Olympia and the girls flew to catch up with him, and when they did, Rachel could see that he was very tired. He was huffing and puffing, and even his spiky hair was starting to droop with exhaustion.

"Please help me!" Jack Frost gasped

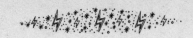

when he saw them. "I'll give you these sneakers if you can get them off my feet so I can rest!"

"It's a deal," Olympia agreed. "Now the only problem is, how do we get the sneakers off?"

The Awards Ceremony

Olympia turned to Rachel and Kirsty. "Any ideas, girls?" she asked hopefully, as Jack Frost ran circles around them.

Kirsty looked down at the super sneakers. It would be impossible to take them off while Jack Frost was running around. But what if his feet weren't on the ground at all?

"I think I have an idea!" Kirsty cried. She fluttered over to Jack Frost. "Can you do a handstand up against that wall over there?"

Jack Frost glared at her. "This is no time for games!" he snapped.

"It's not a game!" Kirsty replied. "If you do a handstand, we'll be able to untie the sneakers and take them off your feet."

"Great idea, Kirsty!" Olympia declared.

Jack Frost ran over to the wall, put his hands down on the ground, and flipped himself up into a handstand. He was still running, but in midair, while holding himself up with his scrawny arms.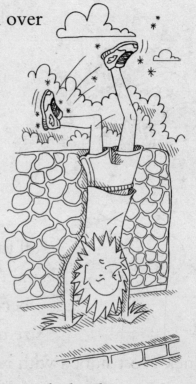

Rachel and Kirsty dodged around Jack Frost's waving feet and untied the laces on both of the super sneakers. Jack Frost wobbled a little, but

managed not to fall over. Then Olympia swooped in. With Rachel and Kirsty's help, she pulled off the left sneaker. It immediately shrank down to its Fairyland size. Next, Olympia and the girls pulled off the right sneaker, and that also shrank, becoming the same size as the other one.

Jack Frost sighed with relief as he flipped himself upright again. "Thank goodness!" He groaned. "I'm going home to take a long rest!" Then he waved his wand and an ice bolt carried

him off to his castle.

"Girls, you were amazing!" Olympia cried. "I couldn't have gotten the sneakers or my other magical objects back without your help. Will you come back  to Fairyland with me again to watch our races?"

"We'd love to, but we'd better not," Rachel said. "Now that the triathlon's over, my mom and dad are probably looking for us."

"Go and enjoy the rest of the awards ceremony, then," Olympia told the girls with a smile.

"I'm sure all your friends in Fairyland will see you again very soon!" Then, holding the super sneakers, she vanished in a sparkling mist of fairy dust.

"Wasn't that the most exciting competition ever?" Rachel said, as she and Kirsty ran hand in hand to watch the awards ceremony.

"I hope we go to many more triathlons," Kirsty replied. "But I don't think we'll ever go to such an amazing one as this, thanks to Olympia and our fairy friends!"

SPECIAL EDITION

There's another fairy adventure
right around the corner!
Join Rachel and Kirsty as they help

Selena
the Sleepover Fairy!

Read on for a special sneak peek. . . .

School Trip

"I feel like it's my birthday and Christmas all at the same time!" said Rachel Walker, bouncing up and down on her seat. "I can't believe we're actually going to a sleepover at the National Museum!"

"It makes it twice as exciting that

you're here," her best friend, Kirsty Tate, agreed, settling down beside her. "It was so nice of the principal to let you come."

Kirsty's school had won a place in a giant charity sleepover, which was being held in the National Museum. Thirty children from the school were going to the city to participate. Rachel was staying with Kirsty for the weekend, so she had been allowed to join in, too.

The bus driver took his seat and the engine rumbled into life. As the bus pulled out of the school parking lot, the girls waved good-bye to Kirsty's mom, who had come to see them off.

"I hope it's not spooky there at night," said a girl named Hannah, who was sitting in the seat behind Rachel. "I'm a little scared of the dark."

"Don't worry," said Kirsty with a

comforting smile. "I've been there before and it's really cool. There are lots of amazing things to do."

"I want to see the Dinosaur Gallery!" said Rachel, opening a bag of candy and passing it around.

"Oh, yes. And the diamond exhibition with all the sparkling jewels," Kirsty added, taking a pink candy and popping it into her mouth.

"The marine fossils!" said Arthur.

"The wildlife garden!" said Allie.

Suddenly there was a loud bang from beneath their feet.

"What was that?" Hannah squealed. "Did a wheel come off?"

"I don't think so," said Rachel, frowning. "It sounded like it was inside the bus. . . ."

RAINBOW magic™

There's Magic in Every Series!

The Rainbow Fairies

The Weather Fairies

The Jewel Fairies

The Pet Fairies

The Fun Day Fairies

The Petal Fairies

The Dance Fairies

The Music Fairies

The Sports Fairies

The Party Fairies

The Ocean Fairies

The Night Fairies

The Magical Animal Fairies

Read them all!

■ SCHOLASTIC

www.scholastic.com

www.rainbowmagiconline.com

HIT entertainment

RMFAIRY5